Town
Murder

Asheville Cozy Mysteries

Book One

By

Patti Benning

Author's Note: On the next page, you'll find out how to access all of my books easily, as well as locate books by best-selling author, Summer Prescott. I'd love to hear your thoughts on my books, the storylines, and anything else that you'd like to comment on – reader feedback is very important to me. Please see the following page for my publisher's contact information. If you'd like to be on her list of "folks to contact" with updates, release and sales notifications, etc…just shoot her an email and let her know. Thanks for reading!

Also…

…if you're looking for more great reads, from me and Summer, check out the Summer Prescott Publishing Book Catalog:

http://summerprescottbooks.com/book-catalog/ for some truly delicious stories.

Contact Info for Summer Prescott Publishing:

Twitter: @summerprescott1

Blog and Book Catalog:
http://summerprescottbooks.com

Email: summer.prescott.cozies@gmail.com

And…look up The Summer Prescott Fan Page and Summer Prescott Publishing Page on Facebook – let's be friends!

To sign up for our fun and exciting newsletter, which will give you opportunities to win prizes and swag, enter contests, and be the first to know about New Releases, click here:
https://forms.aweber.com/form/02/1682036602.htm

TABLE OF CONTENTS

SMALL TOWN
MURDER

Asheville Cozy Mysteries

Book One

CHAPTER ONE

Autumn Roth pulled the smoking pan out of the oven, letting it drop onto the stovetop along with the dishtowel that she had used as a makeshift oven mitt. "Ow, ow, ow," she said, dancing over to the sink and thrusting her hand under the cold water.

"This is all your fault, Frankie, for chewing up the real oven mitt," she said, looking down at her dog. The little terrier was sitting in the middle of the kitchen floor, her stumpy tail wagging happily at all of the commotion. Her wiry blonde fur stuck out in all directions, making her look as if she had just licked an electrical outlet. She didn't look the slightest bit ashamed of herself, which wasn't surprising. The terrier lived for mischief.

Autumn turned off the water and dried her hands on a clean towel. She eyed the mess on the pan. The steaks themselves looked fine, but the foil was still smoking from where the grease had caught fire. She had been trying to save herself some cleaning, and instead had almost caught her house on fire.

"Well, at least flame-roasted steak sounds fancy," she said. "Brandon probably won't even notice. And the pasta salad turned out well. Now all that's left is the dinner rolls — and dessert, of course."

She continued chatting to Frankie as she pulled the frozen dinner rolls out and began to line them up on a clean pan. She had always been a chatterbox, and that wasn't something that she could just turn off when she was alone. At least having the dog there made her feel a little bit less crazy.

The dinner that evening was important to her, and she wasn't about to let the near-disaster with the steaks get her down. She and Brandon had been seeing each other for exactly a year. Ever since he had told her that he just wanted a quiet meal at home together for their anniversary, her dreams had been filled with the sound of wedding bells. He *knew* she didn't want a public proposal. This evening together at her house would be the perfect time for the two of them to get engaged.

In her mid-thirties, Autumn felt the pressure as her biological clock ran toward its expiration date. She wanted kids and a husband, the whole shebang. Watching her niece and nephew grow up had only made her want that life all the more. Brandon might not be the fairytale prince she had dreamed of as a child, but he was kind and responsible, and most importantly, he was interested in her.

Autumn opened the oven to let it air out, then opened the kitchen window a crack to help her house clear of smoke. She checked the clock, then left the kitchen with Frankie at her heels. He would be here soon, and she wanted to freshen up.

She had just finished primping her hair in the bathroom when she heard a knock at the door. Frankie took off like a bolt of lightning, barking frantically. Autumn hurried back into the kitchen and unlocked the door, welcoming Brandon in over the yapping.

"Settle down, Frankie," she said, exasperated. "You know who it is. Sorry, I swear she'll get used to you eventually."

"It's okay," Brandon said as he pushed the door shut behind him. "How are you doing?"

"Great," she said, beaming at him. "I visited my aunt and uncle earlier, and they're both doing well. I spent the afternoon cooking for our dinner tonight."

"I told you not to go to any trouble," he said. "I just want to talk."

"It's no trouble. You know I love cooking. Here, let me take your coat."

She brushed the snow off of it and hung it up in the little closet by the door. While he took his boots off, she cracked open the oven to check on the rolls. They were almost done.

"Go ahead and sit down, I'll bring the food out."

"Autumn, I —"

"It's getting cold. I put the steaks in too early, I should have cooked them last. Go on, sit down."

He vanished into the other room while she bustled around, putting the steaks on plates and taking the bowl of pasta salad out of the fridge. She carried the food out to the dining room, then returned to the kitchen for the bottle of wine she had bought earlier that day. She checked the rolls once more, but they still weren't ready. She would just have to remember to get them out in a few minutes.

At last, she sat down at the table across from Brandon. Smiling at him, she poured herself a glass of wine and passed the bottle to him. He put it down on the table.

"What's wrong?"

"I told you not to go to all of this trouble," he said.

"It wasn't any trouble," she said. "I wanted to do this. For us. Can you believe it's already been a year?"

He sighed. "This is exactly what I wanted to avoid."

"What do you mean?"

"Autumn, I told you I didn't want to do anything for our anniversary. All I was going to do tonight was stop by, so we could talk. I didn't know you were going to make such a big production out of all of this. It's just making it harder."

She felt her stomach twist, but she forced herself to keep smiling. "Making what harder?"

"I don't think we should see each other anymore, Autumn. We can be friends, but that's it. That's all I want."

Autumn was floored. She had been expecting for him to propose, not… this. Things had been going well, hadn't they? They had fun together, they never argued, they liked the same things. She had thought that he was as happy as she was.

"Brandon, I —"

"No, let me keep talking," he said, interrupting her. "I want to say this before you get mad at me. I know it's cliché, but this has nothing to do with you. It's me. I'm just not ready for a committed relationship like this. I know that you want more, but I don't. It isn't fair to you if I keep leading you on. I care about you enough that I want you to be free to go and find someone who is really right for you."

She stared at him, trying to gather her emotions and thoughts before she spoke. She did not want to cry. Not in front of him.

"Okay," she managed at last. "I think you should go now. I need some time by myself."

"Are you going to be okay? I don't want to leave you here alone if you're upset."

"Please, just go."

He got up slowly, looking at her with concern in his eyes. When she ignored him, he pushed his chair in and walked into the kitchen. She heard the closet door open and shut, then stomping as he put on his boots. A moment later, the front door shut behind him, and she was alone at last. She closed her eyes. She had never been more shocked in her life. Just when she had thought things were going so well, he had broken up with her. How could she have been so wrong?

The scent of something burning made her open her eyes again. The dinner rolls. She had forgotten all about them. She rushed into the kitchen and took the pan out of the oven. The rolls were blackened and smoking. Just like her relationship, they were trash.

CHAPTER TWO

Autumn spent the rest of the evening feeling sorry for herself. Her emotions were still too raw for her to take comfort in telling anyone. Brandon had been a part of her life for a year. Now, he was just... gone. Even the coming Christmas festivities seemed dampened now that she knew that she would be spending the holiday alone.

Well, maybe not alone, but without the man who she thought would be the love of her life. She knew her aunt and uncle would be glad to have her over for Christmas dinner, and although spending the evening in an assisted living home might not be what she had planned on, at least she would be spending it with people who cared about her.

She didn't feel any better the next morning, but she didn't feel any worse either. As she got ready for work, she wondered if maybe she hadn't been as invested in her relationship with Brandon as she had thought. Her heart was still heavy, but most of her thoughts seemed centered around the knowledge that her dream of marriage and raising a family would be put on hold for even longer, rather than focused on the new Brandon-shaped hole in her life.

"What if he was right?" she asked Frankie as she brushed her teeth. "Maybe we really weren't right for each other, and he's the only one that could see it. I was so blinded by everything that I wanted that I didn't stop to think that he might not be the one that I wanted it with."

Despite her words, she didn't feel much better as she left the house for Green River Grocery, the store that she managed. Located along the river for which it had been named – which was usually more of a muddy brown than green – the tiny store had been there for longer than she had been alive. If she had been willing to move, maybe she'd have been doing something more meaningful with her life but she loved Asheville. She had lived there for almost ten years, and even though almost nothing had gone as she had planned, the town had become her home.

"Good morning, Jeb," she said as she pushed through the familiar doors, glad to be out of the cold. It was snowing lightly outside, and if the forecast was right, the snowfall would only get heavier toward evening. It was a good thing that she didn't live too far away. Her little two-door car couldn't handle the slick, icy roads very well.

"Is it just me, or are you looking down?" the store's owner asked.

"It's just the holiday blues," she said, offering him a small smile. Jeb was in his fifties, and had taken over the ownership of Green River Grocery when his father had retired. He was in the store daily, but left most of the management of the employees and helping the customers to her. He was a friendly, but shy man, and preferred stocking goods and taking inventory to interacting with other people.

He sighed, straightening up from the box of flavored water that he was unpacking. "Well, what I'm about to tell you won't cheer you up any."

"What is it?" she asked.

"Green River Grocery is going out of business," he said. "We've been in the red ever since that One-Stop Supermarket opened up just outside of town."

"I'm sure people will start shopping here again," she said. "This store's been here since before I was born. It can't close down."

Where would I work? she thought, but didn't say. If Green River Grocery closed permanently, she wasn't the only one that would be out of a job.

"I don't have a choice," he said, his eyes sad. "I just can't afford to keep it open anymore. One-Stop has lower prices, more variety, it's open longer hours, and it's only twenty minutes away. I don't blame people for doing most of their shopping there. I've been trying to think of solutions for months, but the simple fact is, if I keep the store open, I'm going to go broke, and I have a family to consider."

"When?" she asked, feeling just as stunned and lost as she had the night before.

"The end of January," he said. "I was planning on telling everyone after the holidays."

"Why are you telling me now?"

"Most of the other employees other than you are either high schoolers, or retired, and doing this is a part-time job to make some extra cash. You're the only one that's paid a salary, and I know this is your main source of income. I wanted to give you extra time to find somewhere else to work before I shut the doors for good."

"You want me to keep this from the others?"

He sighed. "Do what you think is best. You're better with people than I am. I thought it would be nice for them to enjoy Christmas without worrying, but if you think they should know now, go ahead."

She stared at him, feeling anger – true anger – for the first time in a long while. How could he put this on her? This was his store. If he was making the decision to close it, it was his job to tell the people who worked for him. Why did she have to be the one to decide whether to wreck everyone else's holidays, or let them spend money that they didn't have?

"Anyway, I'm just going to finish restocking the flavored water, then I'm going to get out of here. Let me know if you need references for any jobs. You've been a great manager, and I'm sure you'll be great at whatever you do next too."

To keep herself from saying something she might regret later, Autumn spent the next half hour on the other side of the store until she saw Jeb leave. In less than twenty-four hours, her life had been completely turned on its head. She was single, and in less than two months, she would be out of a job and her only source of income. Her mother had always told her that bad things came in threes, and she couldn't help but wonder what would happen next.

CHAPTER THREE

After her shift, Autumn went to visit the two people who always seemed to make her feel better. Her aunt and uncle lived together at the local assisted living home. After her aunt's stroke, her uncle, who had lost a leg during his time in the military, had been unable to care for her. Since he wouldn't have been capable of taking care of her in their home alone, he had decided to move with her into the assisted living home.

They were both originally from downstate, but had chosen this facility specifically to be near Autumn. She enjoyed their company, and visited them a couple of times every week. Her mother lived across the country, so she was really the only family they had in the area. Neither of them had ever had kids.

"Autumn, I wasn't expecting to see you. Come over here, let me give you a hug."

"Hi, Uncle Albert," she said, embracing the older man. "I know I was just here yesterday, but I could use the company. How is Aunt Lucy doing?"

"She's with the doctor now. They are reviewing her medicines. She should be out in a little bit. Are you going to stay for dinner? I'll go tell the cook."

"Oh, I didn't call ahead. I don't want to be a burden."

"Nonsense, he always makes extra anyway. You sit down, I'll be right back."

Feeling guilty, Autumn took a seat in the armchair in the common area while her uncle made his way toward the dining room and attached kitchen. She always felt bad when he did something that she could do herself, but at the same time, she knew that he valued what independence he had. Making him sit while she went to talk to the cook would do nothing but insult him.

"Hi," she said to the older woman who was sitting a few chairs away. "Mrs. Zimmer, isn't it?"

The other woman nodded and offered her a smile. Autumn grinned back at her. She was getting good at remembering names.

Asheville Meadows was a small facility, but comfortable. From everything Autumn had seen, the staff cared about their jobs, and everyone was treated well. She always enjoyed visiting, but at the same time, it often saddened her. She was one of the few people who visited regularly. Some of the people who lived there had families that only visited on the holidays, and others didn't even have that.

Over the past couple of years, she had grown familiar with both the staff and the residents. Sometimes it is a difficult community to be a part of. Whenever she saw a new face, she knew that it meant that one of the old residents was no longer there. Occasionally they left to move in with family, but most of the time their absence meant that they had passed away. She admired the staff for having the emotional stamina to continue working there, after losing people repeatedly.

She saw her uncle was on his way back, and rose from her seat in case he needed help. He didn't; he had had decades to get used to moving around on crutches. He settled into a chair next to the one that she had sat in and let out a sigh as he leaned his crutches against the arm.

"You're in luck. We have creamy chicken casserole tonight. One of my favorite meals. Cook Benson said that there's plenty for visitors. You are welcome to stay if you would like. You know your aunt and I are always happy to have you here."

"Thanks, Uncle Albert," she said. "It will be nice to have some company for dinner tonight."

"You know I am thrilled to have you visit, but I have a feeling that there is more behind this than just wanting to see us again. Did something happen?"

"Yes," she said. "I'm losing my job. The grocery store is closing, and I don't know what I'm going to do." She leaned her head back against the chair and sighed. "And Brandon ended things."

"I'm sorry," her uncle said. "I liked him. But it's better to be alone than to be with someone who's not right for you."

"I know that in my mind," she said. "But it's a lot more difficult to make my heart understand."

"Your heart will catch up," he said, patting her arm. "And don't worry about your job. I'm sure there's plenty of other things out there for a bright young woman like you."

She smiled. "Thirty-five – almost thirty-six – isn't exactly what I would call being a young woman."

"You're forty years younger than me. I'm going to keep on calling you a young woman. Have you looked into working anywhere else yet?"

"Not yet," she said. "I just found out at the beginning of my shift. It's closing at the end of January, so I have some time. I don't even know where to begin looking if I'm being honest. This is a small town. Most of the jobs that will be hiring in the middle of winter are part-time, for little pay. I would have to take two or three just to support myself."

"What about that big store that opened a few months ago? They must be hiring."

She made a face. "I'm not going to work for the One-Stop Supermarket. They are the reason Green River Grocery is closing down. I'll find something else, or I'll just work multiple jobs."

"If you need to move for work, you do that. Don't worry about me and your aunt. We're fine here."

"I don't want to leave," she said. "Asheville is my home. I have friends here, and you guys, and I don't want to start over."

"I'm just saying, if you do, don't worry about us."

"Thanks, Uncle Albert," she said. "It looks like Aunt Lucy's done with the doctor. I'll help her over."

She rose and walked over to her aunt, who is being pushed along in her wheelchair by one of the staff. She took over, wheeling her towards where her uncle was sitting. They had almost made it when she heard a loud clattering come from the kitchen. There was shouting; it sounded like someone was in trouble. Quickly putting the wheelchair's brakes on, she turned and ran towards the sound.

She stumbled to a halt at the door to the kitchen. Pots and pans were everywhere; steaming food was splattered across the floor. Lying in the middle of the kitchen was a man who was wearing an apron and a white cook's hat. Cook Benson. She had first met him six months before.

"What happened?" she asked.

"I don't know," wailed one of the staff members who was kneeling beside him. "He clutched his throat and then just collapsed. He isn't breathing. Oh, my goodness."

The other woman was giving the man CPR, but he didn't seem to be responding. Autumn could hear someone behind her on the phone, talking frantically to the emergency dispatcher. She stared down at the cook, feeling helpless. His face, she noticed, was red and blotchy, and there were hives on his neck. Had he come into contact with something he was allergic to?

"EpiPen?" she suggested, too quietly. Clearing her throat, she repeated the word, more loudly. The woman who wasn't giving him CPR looked up at her. Something seemed to connect in her mind, and she got up and began patting his pockets. Autumn saw a jacket hanging on the other side of the room and hurried toward it. A quick search of the pockets, and she found the box that the epinephrine injection should have been in. She opened it. It was empty.

CHAPTER FOUR

Autumn stood in the corner of the dining room, watching in equal parts horror and fascination as the police and paramedics swarmed in the kitchen. The paramedics were hurrying to try to stabilize the poor man, but she thought it was already too late. He hadn't been breathing for the entire time that it took the ambulance to get there. He hadn't responded to CPR, at least not as far as she could see. The entire assisted living home was in chaos. One of the nurses was crying. The doctor on staff was arguing angrily with a police officer, who was trying to calm her down.

Autumn was in shock. She had never witnessed anything like this before. It was an emergency – a true emergency – and she had frozen up uselessly. *But what could I have done?* she wondered.

Certainly no more than the staff that was trained in first aid.

She heard someone bark an order, and officers cleared a path to the dining room. The paramedics rolled out a stretcher with a shrouded form on it. She looked away. She couldn't believe that she had just witnessed someone's death.

"Ma'am?" someone said. "Pardon me, but I need to take your statement."

She turned to find a young officer standing at her shoulder. He had a pen and a pad of paper out. He was a good fifteen years younger than her, probably just out of the academy. He was nervous, and she felt bad for him.

"What you need to know?" she asked.

"Just tell me what happened. Anything you can remember. And, um, I'll also need your phone number and to see your ID, in case we need to contact you again."

She closed her eyes and took a deep breath, trying to organize her thoughts. When she opened them, she started from the beginning.

She stayed at the assisted living home for another hour, making sure that her aunt and uncle were settled in their room before she left. The police and paramedics had gone already, and the mood in the building was subdued. She put on her coat and grabbed her purse, feeling tired and saddened, and in need of a warm bath. With dinner wrecked and the kitchen a crime scene, the home was ordering pizza for the residents, but she wasn't staying for that. The last few days had been too much for her. She wanted to go hide in her house, and not come out until things were better.

"The keys weren't there, I swear," she heard a woman say. She paused, feet away from the open door that led to the administrative office. It had the sound of a private conversation, but she couldn't seem to help herself from eavesdropping.

"Justine, the keys are right there, where they always are," a male voice said. "I'm sorry. I know that it was an emergency, and you probably just overlooked them, but it cost a man his life. I'm going to have to let you go."

"Please, Nick, I moved to this town for this job. I love what I do. I take great care of everyone here."

"I'm sorry," he said, and to Autumn's ears, he sounded like he really was. "But I have to think of our residents. What if this was one of them? What happened to Benson was horrible, but we have emergencies almost every week. People go into cardiac arrest, they have strokes, they take falls, and for that we need someone who can keep their mind in an emergency. I know you must feel horrible about this, but I just can't let you keep working here. I'm going to put you on administrative leave with pay until after Christmas. We'll see what the police investigation turns up. But unless they find something that overturns the evidence in front of my eyes, I just can't have you here anymore."

The woman let out a sob, and Autumn stepped back quickly as she rushed out the door. She recognized the doctor; she had been arguing with one of the officers earlier. Justine didn't even glance at her as she rushed towards the front door, trying desperately to keep her composure until she was outside.

"Can I help you?" a tired voice asked. She looked up to see the director of the assisted living home, Nicholas Holt. He ran his hand across his face, sighing. He looked exhausted.

"Sorry, no, I was just on the way out."

"Autumn, isn't it? You're related to the Ottos?"

"Yes, I'm their niece," she said.

"Were you here when the cook collapsed?"

She nodded. "It was horrible. I wanted to help somehow, but there wasn't anything I could do."

"Can I talk to you for a moment?"

She hesitated, thinking of the familiar comfort of her house, but then agreed. She followed him into the office, where he shut the door behind him.

"I already gave my statement to the police," she said.

"I know. I'm sorry, but I just want to ask you something." His eyes darted to the wall behind her. She turned and saw a row of hooks, from which hung various keys.

"What is it?" she asked.

"As I'm sure you know, he wasn't carrying his EpiPen with him," he said. "We have epinephrine here that is prescribed to some of our other residents. Of course, it is against policy to give a prescription to someone it doesn't belong to, but in this case, the use of someone else's EpiPen would've saved his life. We keep the drugs in the medicine closet, and the key stays in here. When I came in here after the police left, I found the key to the medical supply closet hanging where it always is, but Justine swore to me and the police that when she went to find the keys, they were missing. I was just wondering if you saw her at all during what happened, and if you might remember what she was doing."

"I don't think I saw her," she said. "I know that she was visiting with my aunt right before this happened, but I don't know what she did when the cook collapsed. I wish I could help you more. Everything just happened so quickly, it's all a blur. Why? Do you think she was lying about the key?"

"I don't know if she was lying, but I do know that she was mistaken. The key is hanging right there. When she told me what happened, I thought they might have been stolen and I rushed over, but here it was." He shook his head. "I almost wish that she was right, that someone had stolen the key, because the alternative is that she killed a man because she panicked."

Autumn stared at him. He shouldn't be telling her this. He hardly knew her, but she understood that he was in shock too. "I'm sorry," she said. "I wish I could say something that might clear matters up, but I can't. I did see her arguing with one of the police officers earlier, but I don't know what she was doing before that."

"Unfortunately for her, there will be an investigation. She's only worked here for about a year. I personally don't think she meant to do anything wrong, and I hate to see her go through a criminal investigation right after all of this, but there's no way around it. I have to do what is right by my residents, and if she loses her mind in a situation like this, then she's not the right person to work here. We'll have to find another doctor. I can't take the chance of this happening again, and risk someone else suffering for it." He gave her a tight smile. "Sorry. I'm sure you want to get out of here. I guess I just needed someone to talk to. Don't mention what I said about Justine, okay? She's going to have a hard enough time as it is, without any rumors being spread around town."

"Of course," Autumn said. "I won't say anything. I hope you get everything figured out. For what it's worth, this place has been great for my aunt and uncle."

"Thank you," he said. "You don't know what that means to me. I started working here because I wanted to make a difference. I've seen what happens in some homes that aren't run correctly, and it's not pretty. We may not be a huge facility, but I try hard to make sure that everyone gets good care, and that we have employees that are passionate about what they're doing. Feel free to come see me if you ever have any complaints, or just want to talk."

She let herself out of the room, thinking about what he had said. It hadn't crossed her mind until now that the cook's death might not have been an accident. Now, as she thought of the empty EpiPen case, she began to wonder. It didn't make sense that he would carry the empty case around with him without getting a refill. Had someone stolen his prescription from him just before he died?

PATTI BENNING

CHAPTER FIVE

After the worst weekend of her life, Autumn was still feeling down Monday morning. She had to be at the grocery store by ten, but part of her wondered, what was the point? Maybe she should just quit now, and use the next month to job hunt.

She knew that she would never do that, though. Jeb was a good man, and she didn't want to let him down. She didn't know how she would face the employees that morning. Should she tell them before Christmas or not? Witnessing the cook's death the day before had chased that predicament from her mind, but now it was back full force. She didn't know which choice was the right one. To tell them, or not to tell them?

She decided not to mention it that day. Looking at the cheery faces of her employees, it was hard to even think of breaking the news to them. She could always tell them tomorrow, or the next day, or the next, and let them enjoy the coming holiday season for as long as they could. She didn't want to burden anyone else with the knowledge that she had, not until she had to.

After work, she drove straight to Asheville's one coffee shop, the Cocoa and Coffee Café, where she was supposed to meet her best friend, Alicia. Alicia had worked at the store with Autumn, but had left the year before after she had gotten married. She had started working out of her home, making and selling jewelry, and hoping for a baby, a life that Autumn envied. Alicia was a perpetually cheery person, always optimistic, and she was just who Autumn wanted to talk to. If anyone would have answers to her problems, it would be her.

The snow had continued overnight, but had stopped early that morning. The roads in town had all been plowed and salted, and she winced as the car in front of her made slush splatter onto her windshield. She would have to take the vehicle through the car wash sometime that week. All of the salt on the Michigan roads in winter was terrible for vehicles. She had already found two small rust spots on her car, and didn't want to find anymore.

She pulled in the parking lot and shut off her engine, grabbing her purse off of the passenger seat before getting out. It was a cold day, but not windy. The coffee shop had Christmas lights up and in the window hung a banner that wished passers-by a happy holiday. The sight of the decorations helped cheer her up a little. She had always loved the entire Christmas season, though once the holiday was over, she knew that the rest of winter would be a long, dreary wait until spring.

Alicia was already there, sipping a coffee and scrolling through her phone. Autumn ordered a peppermint mocha at the counter, then walked over and joined her friend.

"There you are," Alicia said, looking up and beaming at her. "I didn't even see you walk in."

"Have you been here for long?"

"Not too long," she said. "I was expecting the roads to be worse, so I got here early. How are you? On the phone, you sounded like you had something on your mind. Did Brandon finally pop the question?" She peered at Autumn's hand, looking for a ring.

"No," she replied, sighing. "That's one of the things I wanted to talk to you about. He dumped me."

"No." Alicia stared at her. "What happened? I thought the two of you were doing well."

"I thought so too," she said. "It turns out, we weren't. He gave me the whole, it's not you it's me speech, and said he wanted to be friends, but that's all."

"He's a jerk," her friend said decisively.

Autumn smiled slightly at that. "Just a couple of days ago, you were talking about how he was the best guy I had ever dated, and I needed to hang on to him."

"Well, now he's a jerk. You can do better. Besides, you weren't really in love with him, were you?"

"What do you mean? Of course I was."

Her friend shook her head slowly. "I don't think you were. I think you liked him, and maybe loved the idea of what you might have together in the future, but I don't think you were ever really in love with him. Not like I am with Rory. You never talked about him much unless I asked, and you know I can't shut up about my own husband. And when we went on that trip last year, you didn't seem to miss him at all. If Rory left me, I would be a complete wreck. But looking at you, well, it doesn't look like you were up all night sobbing into your pillow."

"It's not just Brandon," Autumn said. "So much else happened too. This weekend was just so insane. I've hardly had time to process it all."

"What else happened?" her friend asked.

"Jeb is going to close the store," she said softly. "Ever since the One-Stop Supermarket opened up, I guess he just hasn't been making any money off of it. It's closing in January."

"Oh, Autumn, that's horrible. What are you going to do? Where is everyone going to work?"

"I have no idea," she said. "And the thing is, I'm the only one that knows. He told me because he knows I support myself off of this job. He's planning on telling everyone else after the holidays – rather, he wants me to do it for him – so they will be able to enjoy this time with their families."

"That's not right," Alicia said. "They should know. Even if it's just a part-time job for most of them, that doesn't mean they don't need the money."

"I know," Autumn said. "He said I can tell them sooner if I want to. I just… I don't know. I don't know if I should or not, and it's driving me crazy. Then, of course, there's what happened at the assisted living home…"

"Are your aunt and uncle okay?"

"Yes, they're fine, thank goodness. One of the cooks that works there had an allergic reaction to something, and he died."

"Wow," Alicia said, sitting back. "That's terrible."

"I know. And that's not all. I looked in the pocket of his jacket for his EpiPen, and I found a case, but there were no syringes inside. It was empty. And there's the whole thing with the doctor and the keys…"

"What are you talking about? What doctor, and what keys?"

Autumn shut her mouth, realizing what she had let slip. She had promised Nick that she wouldn't tell anyone but Alicia was her best friend and wouldn't tell anyone else.

"Autumn?"

She sighed. It was out of the bag now, anyway. "Don't tell anyone, but the doctor that works there claims that she couldn't find the key to the medicine closet where they keep the other EpiPen's, but when the director went to look for the key afterward, it was hanging in its usual spot. He thinks that she missed them in her panic, but it was a mistake that cost someone his life. He's firing her."

Alicia's eyes were wide. "That's insane. Your weekend sounds like it was a disaster. I'm so sorry. That poor doctor. Can you imagine how guilty she must feel?"

 "I know," she said. "It's like everything imploded. I don't know what they're going to do until they can hire someone else. The other cook is on a two-month long leave. Her daughter was just born."

"They're looking for a new cook, and you're looking for a job," her friend said.

"I can't work there," Autumn said, laughing. "I like to cook as a hobby, but I don't have any actual training or experience."

"I doubt they care," Alicia said. "You could volunteer just for the holiday season. Then if you do well enough, you might be able to stay on long-term. This could be a way to make your dream come true. You've always wanted to have a restaurant."

"It's not exactly a restaurant," she pointed out. "But maybe I will offer to volunteer. I'm not going to quit my job at the grocery store yet, so I can't work there full-time, but I could stop in and make dinners, especially if someone showed me the ropes. With Brandon leaving me, I could use something to keep me busy until after the holidays."

"I'm sure things will start looking up. I mean, they couldn't really get much worse, could they? And about Brandon, I think it's a good thing that he left. You want to be with someone you really love. To make a marriage work, there has to be something special there. It's better to not get married at all than to marry the wrong person."

Autumn gave her friend a grateful smile. What she was saying sounded a lot like what her uncle had said, and she thought that it was probably true. She wanted to get married, but she wanted to do it right. The truth was, she probably hadn't been as in love with Brandon as she thought she was. She would just have to keep believing that there was someone else out there for her.

PATTI BENNING

CHAPTER SIX

"Thank you for doing this. You don't know how much it means to them. To all of us, really."

Autumn smiled at the young woman who was leading her to the kitchen. She had been tasked with showing Autumn around the kitchen and explaining the instructions for the meals.

"I feel so bad for what happened," she said. "Benson's death must have been a shock to everyone. I know the staff here has full schedules, and trying to make meals on top of that must be hard. My aunt and uncle love this place, and it's been great for them, so I'm happy to help however I can."

"Mr. Holt is already gathering applications for the position, but he probably won't hire anyone until the new year. The holiday season is just so busy, and not many people are looking for jobs a week or two before Christmas. Not permanent ones, anyway. It's hard to find someone who wants to work for the salary that we can offer, most of the really skilled cooks can make a lot more money running their own restaurant, and he also doesn't want to hire someone who's just looking for an easy job. Cook Benson actually wanted to volunteer his time here, but Mr. Holt insisted on paying him."

"Do you know if the police figured out what happened?" It had only been a few days since the man's death, but life at the assisted living home had to go on. The residents still needed care, and they needed to eat. While Autumn wasn't a highly trained cook, she had always enjoyed cooking, and unlike the staff members who had been pitching in in the kitchen for the past few days, she would be able to dedicate her time here without letting other responsibilities go by the wayside.

"I have no idea," the young woman said, shaking her head. Her name was Natalie, and to Autumn she looked like she was just out of high school. "One of the nurses quit, and another staff member left as well, because they think he was killed on purpose. I don't know where the rumor came from, but I've heard people saying that it's the doctor who did it."

She lowered her voice for the last sentence. Autumn frowned. The only person that she had mentioned anything to was Alicia, but her friend wouldn't have told anyone here. That meant the news of the doctor's administrative leave must have spread faster than expected.

"What have you heard?" she asked, wondering how much the young woman knew.

"Just that she's the one that was supposed to get the keys to the medicine cabinet, but she never got them. I know it sounds far-fetched – why would she want to kill Cook Benson? – but at the same time, everyone that I've spoken to that was there the day it happened seems to agree that she ran off to get the keys and never came back. I don't know what to think, and I guess it's not any of my business. I'm just here to take care of the residents."

"You're right, it's not something that we need to figure out ourselves. Better to leave that for the police. Right now, I'm more concerned about learning my way around this kitchen."

That was the truth. The assisted living facility's kitchen was much larger than she had remembered, with a cold, almost industrial feel to it. Everything was made out of stainless steel, and it was nothing like her warm, inviting kitchen at home.

"I helped the cook a couple of times," Natalie said. "That's probably why they asked me to show you around. There are thirty residents here, but on the holidays, we have a lot more people because families come to visit. Christmas is going to be pretty busy, so you will probably want to get some helpers too."

"Since you already know your way around, would you like to help me out? I could use your help tonight, too, if you have time."

"I'd love to help you for Christmas dinner, but I can't tonight. My shift ends in three hours, then I have to leave. I'm taking night classes, and the semester ends next week, so I have a lot of studying to do. You'll be fine, though. Tonight's going to be a quiet night. We don't usually have that many extra guests during the weekdays. It will probably just be the residents here for dinner."

She thought that Natalie was trying to reassure her, but the thought of making dinner for thirty people was overwhelming. She had never cooked for so many people all at once. What had she gotten herself into? She was in over her head.

"This is the menu for the rest of the month. All of the residents get a print out the menu, so you should probably stick to it. Everything should be low-sodium; the residents that don't have to watch their sodium intake can add salt to their meals when it's on the table. There should be a book with all the recipes around here somewhere. Some of the desserts are premade, and we just heat them up, but we try to make everything else from scratch. I know a lot of people complain that the food is bland, but don't pay them any attention. Just follow the recipes and the menu, and things will be all right."

"And what if there are more guests than usual? Will I have to modify the recipes?"

"Yes, but there's a handy chart that will tell you how to adjust the ingredients. You should try to make three to four extra servings for each meal in case someone drops a plate on the floor or a guest arrives unexpectedly."

"Okay," Autumn said. "It looks like tonight is meatloaf, mashed potatoes, green beans, and brownies for dessert?"

"Yep. Here's the recipe book. I think the meatloaf is on page thirty-six. Make sure that you mash the potatoes well, because some of the residents can't chew very well. Before Mr. Holt took over, we used the dried potato mix, but now we have to use real potatoes. It's a bit of a pain, but people like them better, so I suppose it's worth it."

"Where will I find everything I need to start cooking?"

"The potatoes and spices are in the pantry, meat and milk are in the fridge of course. The brownie mix is in the pantry as well, and I think you'll need two or three boxes. Pots and pans will be in the cupboards, other than the ones hanging above the stove. I'm sure you'll be able to find everything, feel free to look around. There's a few hours before dinner, so you have some time to familiarize yourself with the kitchen. Do you think there's anything else you might need?"

"No, I guess not," Autumn said, trying to keep the doubt out of her voice. "It seems pretty self-explanatory. I suppose I'll get started. You go and do what you need to do."

"Good luck. Mr. Holt will be in later today, so if you need anything else, he'll be able to help you."

Natalie gave her a cheery wave then left the kitchen. Autumn stood next to the island that housed the expansive stove range, feeling alone and overwhelmed. She told herself that she was only going to be doing this a couple of days a week until Christmas. It was the right thing to do. It wasn't like she had anything better to do with her time, anyway. At least this way, she would be making a difference, and it would also give her something to take her mind off of the mess that her life had become.

"Potatoes," she said, looking down at the recipe book. "Let's start with those."

It took her the better part of an hour to first find the bowls, knives, and peeler, and then wash and peel the potatoes by hand. By the time the potatoes were cubed and ready to be boiled, she sorely needed a break. She made her way to the bathroom. After using the facilities, she washed her hands and stared at herself in the mirror. She didn't feel quite so overwhelmed anymore. It had been relaxing to stand at the sink peeling potatoes for an hour. Her mind had been free to wander, but instead of thinking about all the things that had gone wrong, she had been thinking about the future, and what she could do to make it better. First things first, she had decided she needed to find a new job. She didn't have the faintest clue where she would start looking, but was sure that the Internet could help her with that. She should treat this as an opportunity to try to follow her dreams. If she could start work as a sous chef somewhere, she might be able to make enough money to support herself while she got the training she needed to become a real chef, then she could spend the rest of her life doing something that she actually enjoyed.

Feeling a little bit better about the coming months, she returned to the kitchen, greeting Mrs. Zimmer and a couple of other familiar faces on her way. Once in the kitchen, she filled the largest pot she could find with water from the sink and put it on the stove. She was just about to turn on the gas burner when something made her hesitate. She hadn't yet turned the dial, but the air smelled strongly of gas. Something was wrong.

The hair on the back of her neck prickling, she looked down at the stove and saw that all of the dials had already been turned to high. Horrified, she quickly turned them off. They couldn't have been on for the entire hour that she was peeling the potatoes — she would have noticed the smell — which meant that someone must have snuck in and turned them on when she went to the bathroom. Who would do such a thing? Chilled, she realized that this meant that Cook Benson's death hadn't been an accident after all. Someone was actively trying to kill the cooks at the assisted living home.

PATTI BENNING

CHAPTER SEVEN

"Are you sure that you didn't bump the dials, or turn them on and then forget about them?" Nick Holt asked her.

"I'm sure," she said. "I may not have much experience in a large kitchen like this, but I'm not stupid. I know not to turn gas burners on without lighting them."

He shook his head, staring at the stove in the center of the kitchen warily. "I can't believe this. If you had lit one of the burners, the entire kitchen might have burned down. You could have died. This could have destroyed the entire home. Who would do something like this?"

"Maybe one of the residents just got confused?" Natalie suggested. Autumn had run into her when she rushed to Nick's office after turning the burners off.

"It's possible, I suppose," Nick said. "But nothing like this has ever happened before. Natalie, I'm going to ask you to gather the staff. We need to figure out what happened here."

"It can't be a coincidence," Autumn said. Her initial fear had passed, and now she was angry. Someone had tried to kill her, and she was certainly going to take it personally. "First Cook Benson dies, and no one can find an EpiPen for him, then this happens. Someone's trying to kill anyone who works in the kitchen."

"Why would someone want to do that?" Nick asked. "Killing our cooks doesn't achieve anything, other than making the staff more stressed and taking away a member of our team. There's no benefit to stopping the kitchen from working."

"I know it doesn't make sense, but it also doesn't make sense that there would be two accidents, one fatal and one potentially fatal, in the same room in a matter of days. I'm just as happy to believe in coincidences you are, but this is a bit much for me."

"I understand if you don't want to volunteer here any longer," he said. "And trust me, I will be looking into this. I won't let this slide."

"I don't know what I'm going to do yet," Autumn said. "Are you going to call the police?"

He hesitated. "If questioning the staff and residents doesn't turn anything up, then I might," he said. "I don't want to waste their time, though. I know everyone here, and I'll be able to get the truth out of them much more quickly than the police would. We don't have any interior security cameras – all part of trying to make this place feel like a home, not the medical facility that it is. There isn't anything that the police could do that I can't."

"I still think they should know. It might help them with their investigation into Benson's death," she said. He nodded. Glad that he had agreed with her, she continued, saying, "What should I do now? Should I try to finish the meatloaf?"

"You can head home if you want," he said. "I don't think anything in the kitchen should be touched. If I do have to call the police, they might want to dust for fingerprints. If you'd like to stay for dinner, you're free to, of course. We will probably order pizza again. It may not be the healthiest thing in the world, but the residents like it, and it will help distract them from thinking about what almost happened."

Autumn bit her lip, then decided that she had already planned to be here for the evening, so she might as well stay. "I'll stick around for dinner. Let me know if you need any help."

"I will," he said. He looked at her, and she saw surprise in his expression. He hadn't expected her to stay. "Thank you, Autumn. It really means a lot that you're staying to help."

Autumn joined her aunt and uncle, who were in their shared room together. When Uncle Albert saw her, despite her protests, he rose to hug her. Her Aunt Lucy, who was still unable to form clear words, and had limited mobility in her face and her right leg and arm, gave her the best smile she could.

"Hi, Aunt Lucy," Autumn said, bending down to hug her aunt. "It's good to see you."

"Is dinner ready?" her uncle asked, looking at his watch. "It's a bit early."

"No, there won't be any meatloaf tonight," she said. "Something came up."

She told them both all about what had happened.

"Nick thinks it was an accident – that some confused resident went in and did it without knowing what would happen."

"Do you think it was something else," her uncle said. "Do you think someone did it on purpose?"

"How can I not?" She shook her head. "It can't be a coincidence. Not with what happened on Sunday."

"But why would someone try to kill the cook?"

She threw up her hands, then felt bad for taking her exasperation and frustration out on her uncle. "I don't know. All I know about this place is what I hear when I visit you guys. Uncle Albert, do you know anyone that might have some reason to want to disrupt the kitchen? Someone who hates the food here, or hated Benson, or anything like that?"

"Well, the food has never been great," he said with a chuckle. "I know it's not the cook's fault, though. They have to give us all this low-sodium stuff, since a lot of us have issues with blood pressure and cholesterol. Plenty of people complain about it, but I don't think anyone would actually do anything about it. Eating bland food isn't exactly a good reason to commit murder. And Benson was great. He was always happy to laugh, and loved listening to the stories some of the residents told him. He was a good guy. He could have been making a lot more money cooking somewhere else, but he chose to work here. I don't know anyone who would want to see him dead."

Autumn sighed and sat down. Her aunt reached out with her good hand and patted Autumn's arm. She gave her aunt a tight smile. Her emotions were a tangle right now. She was angry at what had happened, frightened by the thought of someone trying to kill her, and frustrated to know that she couldn't do anything about any of it. All she wanted was to have a nice, quiet holiday season, do some good work in her spare time, and find a new job. She didn't want to be involved in whatever was going on here, but at the same time, she couldn't back out now. Not with her aunt and uncle still here. She would make good on her promise to cook some of the dinners, and just be sure to keep her guard up while she was there. She would double check everything before she used it.

About an hour later, someone knocked on the door to her aunt and uncle's room. She got up and opened it to find Nick Holt standing outside with a box of pizza.

"I come bearing dinner," he said. "I was wondering, would you mind if I join the three of you? Everyone's eating in their rooms tonight. The police are here, and they're going through the kitchen now."

Autumn looked over her shoulder to check with her aunt and uncle before she said, "Yes, of course, come on in."

She took the pizza box from him, placing it on the coffee table. Her uncle got up and pulled some paper plates and napkins out of the cupboard. She helped him carry them over to the table, and the four of them settled down to eat.

"So, I take it you didn't find out anything from the staff?" she asked the director.

"Unfortunately, no. None of the staff remember seeing anyone go towards the kitchen, but we are a little bit understaffed as it is. None of the residents were able to help either. Someone suggested that the kitchen was haunted, and now that's the most popular theory going around."

"Better than the rumor about Justine," Autumn said.

He raised an eyebrow.

"Natalie told me that people are saying that she let Benson die on purpose. I don't know how it got started, but I feel bad for her."

"So do I," Nick said. "Telling her that she was being put on administrative leave is one of the hardest things I've ever done. She's a good woman, and I know that she didn't do it on purpose. But at the same time, I have to think about the residents' well-being. At least she's not here to hear the rumors about her. I will have to talk to the staff about it."

"Well, this is the most exciting thing that has happened since we moved in," Uncle Albert said. "Benson's death is terrible, of course, but there is nothing like a good mystery. When you find a new cook, will you tell them about what happened?"

"Yes," Nick said. "I already thought about that. Whoever decides to work here deserves to know the possibility that the incidents are connected. Of course, it will probably take a while to hire someone new. I'm just glad Autumn has agreed to stay on for a while."

"What?" her uncle asked, putting down his slice of pizza. "Autumn, I thought you had more sense than that. You can't stay here and put yourself in danger for us."

"Look, like Nick says, we don't even know if what happened was connected," she said. "Even though I don't think it's a coincidence, that doesn't mean that I am right. I would feel bad if I left and someone else got hurt. I'll just be careful from now on."

"You better be," her uncle said. "I'll keep an eye out for you. I've got some friends here that will help as well. If anyone suspicious gets near the kitchen, you'll know about it."

CHAPTER EIGHT

The next day was one of her rare days off, when Jeb would be managing the day-to-day tasks at the store, and she was free to do whatever she wanted. It was a Thursday; not exactly prime time for going out and having fun, but she didn't mind. After the busy week that she had had, she was glad to be able to just relax on her own with Frankie. The little terrier was perfectly content to lay on her lap while she sat on the couch and caught up with her favorite shows. She reheated leftovers, made some hot chocolate, and even turned on the gas fire in the fireplace. The hiss of the gas reminded her of what had happened the day before, and she felt her mood plummet, even as she sipped her hot cocoa. The police had found nothing. They still had no idea who had done it, or whether it had been on purpose, or an accident. Even worse, she had seen some of the staff looking at her suspiciously when she left the evening before. She didn't know why anyone would suspect her, but was sure that there must be a rumor flying around similar to the one about Justine.

She kept telling herself that she would be perfectly safe when she went back to cook dinner that evening. Even if someone had tried to hurt her before, they wouldn't try it again, not with the police already on alert.

"Okay, that's enough moping around," she said as the credits ran on one of her shows. She got up, Frankie hopping off her lap. Autumn carried her mug into the kitchen and set it in the sink. "Do you want to go for a walk?"

She put on her warmest socks, then pulled on her winter boots and a fluffy parka. She added a wool hat and a scarf to the ensemble, and clipped Frankie's leash to her collar before she put on her gloves. It was cold outside, and flurries of snow were falling from the gray sky. Regardless, it was beautiful. The world outside was a white wonderland. Even though it was daytime, some of her neighbors had their Christmas lights on, and the soft glow made her heart lift. A walk around the block with her dog would be perfect to clear her mind of gloomy thoughts.

She locked the door behind her and started down the sidewalk, her dog sniffing and bounding through the snow. She waved to one of her neighbors, who was shoveling snow off of his driveway. When she got back, she would begin looking for a job. She loved this place, and didn't want to leave it.

She was coming back around the block when she saw someone standing on her porch. Her first thought was that it was one of the police, hopefully coming to clear up what had happened the day before. Then she recognized the car parked in front of her house. It was just Brandon.

She called out to him as she drew nearer. He turned, looking surprised to see her out.

"I thought you were just ignoring me," he said. "I suppose I should have guessed that you weren't in when I didn't hear Frankie barking."

"We just took a walk. I wanted to clear my mind. What are you doing here?"

"I came to apologize," he said. "I want to talk to you. Can we go in? It's freezing out here, and I don't have gloves on."

She nodded, reaching into her pocket for her keys as she tried to sort out how she felt. So much had happened since he had broken up with her, and he hadn't really been at the top of her list of priorities. She supposed that she was glad to see him, and she didn't really harbor any anger toward him. She was much more concerned with the attacks at the assisted living home than with anything he might have to say.

"Come on in," she said. "We can sit in the living room if you'd like. Do you want some hot chocolate? I had some earlier, but if you want, I'd be happy to make some more."

"No thanks," he said. "Actually, on second thought, sure. Why not? 'Tis the season."

She removed her outdoor gear and unclipped Frankie's leash before pouring milk into the kettle on the stove. While it heated up to a simmer, she got out the package of hot chocolate and the mug.

"So, what did you want to talk about?" she asked.

"I guess I just want to see how you're doing," he said. "I called you yesterday, but you ignored me."

"Oh, I was at the assisted living home. I'm volunteering there; cooking dinners on my evenings off."

"That's nice of you," he said.

"Yeah," she said absently as she poured the hot milk into the mug of cocoa.

"Autumn, what's wrong?" he asked, putting his hand on her shoulder.

She bit her lip, wishing he would stop. He had wanted to end it, and it was over. Why couldn't he just leave her be now?

"I just wish the circumstances were different," she said, handing him the mug of hot chocolate.

"What do you mean?" he asked as he followed her into the living room.

"I mean, I wish I wasn't volunteering there because I was covering for someone who died."

"Someone died? What happened?"

She realized that he probably didn't know anything about Benson's death. He had never been much of one for the news, and she didn't even know if the papers would have had anything in them about the death. It had only been a few days ago. How quickly did papers print the obituaries? She sat in the armchair, forcing him to sit on the couch, and told him about the cook's death, and the near disaster with the gas in the kitchen.

"Are you serious, Autumn? You almost died."

"Yeah. So, I've been a bit distracted. Plus, the grocery store is closing down, so I have to find somewhere else to work. This isn't really a great time, Brandon. We can talk later. Let's give it a couple of months, okay?"

"I don't want to give it that long," he said. He wrapped his hands around the mug. "I think I might've made a mistake."

She frowned. On Sunday morning, she might have been glad to hear his words, but so much had happened recently that their breakup was no longer the most important thing on her mind. Witnessing a death and facing the prospect of losing her job had somehow given her the space to see that Alicia was right. She hadn't been in love with Brendan. She cared about him, and she had wanted the future that he might have offered, but it wasn't the sort of romance that she desired.

"I don't think it was a mistake," she said. "You're right. I don't think it was me or you. It was both of us, or neither of us. We just aren't right for each other. No hard feelings, okay? Just let me figure out everything else that is going on, and we can talk again. We can be friends, like you wanted. I would enjoy that. I really did care about you, Brandon. I still do. I enjoyed spending the past year dating you. It was… nice. I had a lot of fun."

He stared at her for a moment, then gave a dry chuckle. "I came here to try to repair things between us. I guess that was silly of me. I'm sorry for hurting you, Autumn."

"Like I said, no hard feelings." Even though she had come to terms with the fact that he wasn't the one for her, thinking about their breakup still stung. She had been so sure that they would get married, and she felt ridiculous to think about how blind she had been.

"I guess I really messed up, huh?" he said. "I'm sorry to bother you. I'll be going now. I want you to be careful, though. Okay? Whatever's going on at the assisted living home, it sounds dangerous. I don't want you to get hurt."

"I'll be careful," she promised. "My aunt and uncle are there, they will watch out for me. Nick also said he would keep an eye out for me and asked the staff to do the same. Someone has to cook the meals, and I really do enjoy it. I will just have to hope that I'm wrong, and everything was a coincidence."

"Nick?"

"Oh, he's the director of the home. He's a good guy. He seems to really care about his job."

"Ah." Brandon fell silent. Autumn frowned.

"What?

"Nothing. It's not my business anymore, I suppose. Here. Sorry I didn't drink much of the hot chocolate." He gave her a tight smile. "I'll see you sometime. I'll talk to you after the holidays."

Puzzled and slightly hurt at his sudden departure, Autumn watched him go. Her emotions were a mess. She knew that Alicia was right. She hadn't been in love with Brandan, and she didn't want to waste her life being married to someone that she didn't really love. At the same time, some small part of her brain wondered if she had done the right thing. Should she have taken him back? Was it time to settle? Was he her last chance at having a family?

CHAPTER NINE

Her relationship troubles were relegated to the back burner by the time that she went into work the next day. Thursday evening, she had successfully cooked dinner for the entire assisted living home. Everything had gone smoothly, and she hadn't felt endangered once. Even better, some of the residents had come forward to compliment her afterward. Not only had she made a meal for thirty people without burning anything, they had liked it enough to thank her.

It was a good feeling, to know that she had done something right. She had thoroughly enjoyed making the meal, and was already looking forward to going back on Saturday to do it again. Before long, it would be Christmas, her favorite day of the year. She would spend most of the day there, preparing the

Christmas feast that they would enjoy together the evening of the holiday. The thought cheered her up even more. She wouldn't have enjoyed sitting at home alone all by herself. Now, she would be spending it with her aunt and uncle, surrounded by the people that she had gotten to know at the assisted living home.

"Hi, Ms. Roth," Grace, one of her employees, said when she got in. Autumn smiled at the younger woman.

"Hi, Grace," she replied. "How are you doing today?"

"Great. I love working at this time of year. Everything just feels so festive. I'm looking forward to the time off around Christmas. I love that Jeb closes the store for Christmas Eve and Christmas Day. A lot of places make their employees work through the holiday now."

"He's a good guy," Autumn said. She frowned, thinking about the store's fate. She hated being the only one that knew about it.

"Is something wrong?" Grace asked her.

"I'm just tired," she replied. She forced herself to smile. "I'm going to go take my coat off, then I'll come back here to help you restock the shelves."

She told herself that she wasn't lying. She *was* tired. She had been up late the night before looking for new jobs.

She managed to keep the secret for the next few hours. She focused on her work, restocking shelves, helping customers find what they needed, and wiping the registers clean periodically throughout the day. In the early afternoon, she was surprised to see a familiar face.

"Nick?" she said.

The director of the assisted living home turned around and gave her a smile. "Autumn. It's a small world. I was just thinking about you." He took in her khaki pants, her green shirt, and her name tag. "Do you work here?"

"Yep," she said. "This is my day job, when I'm not moonlighting at the assisted living home."

"I must have seen you around here before, but I didn't realize it. It's a nice store. I like the owner. His mother was at the home until last year, when she passed away."

Autumn remembered Jeb's mother's funeral. She hadn't realized the older woman had lived at Asheville Meadows.

"Can I help you find anything?" she asked.

"Nope," he said. "I'm just here to pick some groceries up. I should probably start making lists, but I never seem to quite get around to it. I usually just walk the aisles and pick up whatever looks good."

She smiled. "Well, that's one way to do it."

"I'll see you Saturday, right? Some of the residents have family visiting, so it will be a bit of a bigger meal. Are you up to it? You did such a good job last night."

"I'm sure I will manage," she said. "Do you know if Natalie or any of the other staff will be able to help me?"

"Natalie asked me earlier today if she could have a couple of hours off from her normal duties to help. I told her to knock herself out. I can't thank you enough for helping out, Autumn. It really means a lot to everyone there."

"I enjoy it," she said. "I've always loved cooking. When I was younger, I used to dream of opening my own restaurant."

"What's stopping you? You still could."

She frowned. "I don't know about that. I would need the money to get started up, and I don't really have any experience other than the cooking I've done for fun. I mean I suppose I have some experience running a business, thanks to this job. But I don't want to get in over my head. I don't have anyone to help me, and it would be too much to manage on my own."

"I'm pretty sure that you could do it, if you set your mind to it. Or at least, I get that feeling from your aunt and uncle. Your uncle talks very highly of you. They love that you visit so much."

"I know it's what I would want if I were in their shoes," she said. "Family is important. My mom visits when she can, but she lives across the country. My younger sister is only a few hours away, but she is busy with her own family. I figure it's the least I can do."

"It's more than most people do, and I respect that a lot." He gave her a half wave and began to walk away, then hesitated. "I hope this doesn't seem inappropriate, but would you want to go out to dinner with me next week?"

She stared at him, surprised. "Are you asking me on a date?"

"Don't worry, I won't be offended if you say no. I probably shouldn't have asked anyway, I know a lot has been going on lately."

"I would love to," she said, smiling at him.

He returned her smile. "How about Monday?"

"That would be good. We can talk more tomorrow while I am cooking dinner. I'm looking forward to it."

"Me too."

Her heart was lighter than ever as she went about her work. She had been completely blindsided when he asked her out, but now she couldn't stop thinking about him. He was handsome, and from what she had seen, was a kind person. She felt a little bit guilty for moving on from Brandon so quickly, but she told herself that he was the one who had ended it. It wasn't like she was being disloyal to him.

"I'll see you tomorrow," Grace said, approaching Autumn in her coat.

"Have a nice evening," she said. "Drive safely. The roads look like they are getting bad again."

"I will," her employee said cheerily. "Next time you see me, I will be driving a new car. I finally have enough saved up to make a down payment on a vehicle that I have been in love with for the past few months. The payments are bit steep, but it will be worth it. I think I'm up for a raise sometime soon, too."

Autumn froze, her stomach swooping. Grace didn't know that the grocery store was going to shut down. She was planning on having this job for a long time to come. She knew that she couldn't let her employee get tied into a contract with payments that she may not be able to make after January.

"Grace, wait," she said. "There's something I have to tell you."

Her employee turned towards her, her face puzzled. Autumn knew that her tone had been sharp, and she felt even more guilty.

"I'm sorry. I just couldn't let you go out there and make a mistake." She looked around to make sure they were alone, then lowered her voice. "Don't tell anyone else yet, but Jeb is going to close this store for good. It will be closing at the end of January."

The employee stared at her, her eyes wide. "What do you mean?"

"After January, none of us will have jobs. I thought you should know before you make a commitment like buying a car."

"When was he going to tell us?"

"Not until after Christmas," Autumn said. "He didn't want to wreck anyone's holiday."

"Oh, my goodness," the employee said. "Thank you for telling me. I guess… I guess the car will have to wait. I will have to find another job. Where are you going to work?"

"I don't know yet," Autumn said. "I sent in a couple of applications, but I won't know anything for a while. Please, don't tell the others, okay?"

"Why not? They deserve to know too. People need time to find work before this place shuts down."

"I agree. I… I just want time to think about it for a little longer, okay?"

Her employee nodded hesitantly. Autumn watched her go. Her heart was heavy once more. She knew that Grace was right. She had an announcement to make.

CHAPTER TEN

Autumn stood in front of the mirror, looking at herself critically. Her red hair was as tame as it would get, and her makeup did nothing to hide the sprinkle of freckles across her nose, but all in all, she didn't think she looked too bad.

"Get out here, I want to see you," Alicia called from the other room.

"Hold on, give me a second."

She freshened up her lipstick, and smiled at herself. First dates were always exciting. She could remember the first time that she and Brandon had gone out; they had seen a movie, and had gotten coffee afterward. She had liked how gentle and nervous he had been during the evening. He had been nice and unthreatening, and even though she hadn't felt a spark, she had agreed to see him again. Things had gone on from there.

She had no idea what to expect from this evening with Nick. She had only ever seen him at the assisted living home, other than that once at the grocery store. At work, he was always thinking about a million other things, all of which were important. It would be odd to have his attention focused only on her, and it made her nervous. She was surprised at the butterflies in her stomach. She hadn't felt that way about Brandon in a long time, if ever.

"Autumn, come on. You asked me to come over and help you get ready, but all I've done is sit on your couch and pet your dog."

"I'm coming, I'm coming," she replied. She left the bathroom and walked into the living room, standing in front of her friend. Alicia twirled a finger, and Autumn turned around slowly.

"I like it," her friend said. "The dress is a good color on you."

She was wearing a dark green dress that she had dug out of her closet, along with pantyhose and black boots. The boots were required; the snow was coming down heavily, and didn't show any signs of stopping soon.

"You sure it's not too… Christmassy? With my red hair, I always feel like a walking Christmas ornament whenever I wear green."

"Don't be ridiculous. You look hot, and not at all like a Christmas ornament. What necklace are you wearing?"

"It is the one my mom gave me when I moved here." Autumn looked down at the delicate silver four-point compass around her neck. "She said it was to remind me to follow my own path, and not settle for someone else's."

"That is good advice," her friend said. "So, this guy, Nick. What's he like?"

"He's handsome," Autumn said. "And confident. From what I've seen, he tries to treat everyone fairly. I think he has a good heart, even though he has a lot on his plate right now."

"Now the big question," Alicia said. "Why isn't he married?"

Autumn raised her eyebrows. "What do you mean?"

"Well, if he is as handsome and confident as you say, why is he single?"

"Maybe he just hasn't met the right person yet. Just because he's single in his mid-thirties doesn't mean there's something wrong with him. Look at me."

"I didn't mean to offend you," her friend said. "You're right, there is nothing wrong with being single. I guess it's just that I know so many single women who always complained that all the good guys are taken, that whenever someone meets a single guy who seems too good to be true, I always worry that it is."

Autumn wished that Alicia hadn't brought the subject up. Now, she couldn't stop wondering. Why *was* he single? Trying to push the paranoid thoughts out of her mind, she straightened up and looked at the clock. He would be there soon.

"Do you want me to leave?" her friend asked.

"No, you should stay. You can meet him, then we can talk when I get back. There's some wine in the fridge, help yourself. You know how to work the TV. If Frankie has to go out, just put her out back. She won't want to be outside for long, not with the snow."

"A dog after my own heart," the other woman said. "I'm not fond of all of this snow either. I need to live somewhere warmer."

"Don't you dare move away," Autumn said. "You're my best friend, you aren't allowed to go anywhere."

"I suppose I'll stay here just for you," Alicia responded with a grin. "My husband has nothing to do with it, of course."

"Oh, Rory would follow you anywhere," Autumn said.

"Maybe it's a good idea. He and I can move somewhere nice and warm, and you could come with us. You need to switch careers anyway, so you might as well do it somewhere with nicer weather."

"I'm happy here," she said. The truth was, she loved the snow. It was so beautiful, and she loved the changing seasons. She would not want to live somewhere that didn't get snow in the winter.

"I guess I'll keep chugging along here, then," her friend said. "Whatever happened with that guy that died at Asheville Meadows?"

"Nothing," she replied. "As far as I know, it was an accident. The police haven't found anything incriminating. He was allergic to peanut butter, and the kitchen had some peanut butter powder to add to some of the residents' food. A lot of them don't eat as much as they need to, and it is high in protein and calcium. He ingested some, somehow, and that was that."

"It still seems suspicious, doesn't it? What about the lady who didn't get to the key on time?"

"As far as I know, they haven't found anything out about her either. Nick thinks that she just panicked and overlooked the keys. No one has found evidence to contradict him yet."

"So do you feel safe there now? No more weird incidents like when the kitchen almost blew up?"

Autumn hesitated. Nothing else had happened, but a couple of time she had gotten goosebumps while she was in the kitchen, with the feeling that somebody was watching her. Maybe it was ridiculous, but her gut still told her that something there was wrong.

"Nothing else has happened, so I suppose I do," she said at last.

"You don't sound certain," Alicia said.

"It's fine," Autumn said. "I don't think I'm in danger. Even if somebody was trying to kill the cook, it would be too dangerous for them to try again. The police have already been called out twice."

"Okay." Her friend didn't sound convinced, but it appeared that she had decided to let the subject drop. "Do you think you will keep working there after the holidays?"

"I doubt it," she replied. "I'm sure Nick will hire someone more qualified. I have already been looking for other jobs. I have an interview at the feed store later this week."

"The feed store? Will that pay enough?"

"They're looking for a full-time manager, and it includes benefits, so I'm sure I will be able to survive on it. I'll miss the grocery store though. The people there feel like family."

"I'm sure you'll be just as close with the new people wherever you end up working," her friend said. "You're good at that."

Autumn smiled at her, then shot up when she heard the doorbell ring. Frankie took off for the door, barking. "That must be him."

CHAPTER ELEVEN

She saw Nick's eyes light up when she answered the door, and she felt herself blush. He had cleaned up nicely; he was wearing a black button-down shirt and black slacks, with a wool coat over it all. There was a dusting of snow on his shoulders and his hair.

"Are you ready to go?" he asked. "Or do you need a few more minutes? I know I'm a little bit early. Oh, who's this?" He bent down to let Frankie sniff his hands.

"That's Frankie. She barks at everyone, just ignore her. I have to go grab my purse, then we can leave."

She hurried into the living room and took her purse off the coffee table. Alicia followed her back toward the door. Autumn made the introductions, then shooed Frankie back inside and left with Nick.

"Thanks for picking me up," she said.

"I wouldn't want to make you drive through the snow on your own like this," he said. "I don't think your car could handle it."

She followed him toward his SUV, which he had parked alongside the curb. He held the passenger door for her and she got in, admiring the heated leather seats inside.

"This must be nice for snow," she said.

"It also comes in handy when I need to haul something for one of the residents. Not all of them have family that can move furniture for them."

He drove them to the Fresh Harvest Inn, parking close to the door and then holding the passenger door open for her. Autumn smiled as she got out of the car. So far, so good. She was looking forward to dinner. She didn't eat out much on her own, preferring to cook at home or get takeout. Come to think of it, it had been a while since she and Brandon had been on a nice date like this.

"Sorry, our options are a bit limited around here. I figured we shouldn't drive too far, since the snow is supposed to keep coming down."

"I love this place," she said. "They have great food, and the kitchen is run by one of my uncle's friends."

"I know, he stops by the assisted living home pretty often. He's actually one of the first people I called when I realized that we would need a new cook."

"Oh? Is he going to start working at Asheville Meadows?"

"He politely declined," Nick told her. "He said he wanted to stay in his own kitchen, and I understand that."

"I'll keep volunteering there as long as I can," Autumn told him. "I'm not sure what my work schedule will be like coming into the new year, though. I'll be starting a new job soon."

Their conversation paused while they were seated and placed their drink orders. Once the server had walked away from the table, Nick said, "You said you're starting a new job? Where?"

"I'm not sure yet," she said.

"Do you have any leads?"

"I have one. It's just at the feed store, and I'm going in for an interview this week," she said.

"What about your restaurant?"

She smiled. "That is just a silly dream. I need something that will actually make money."

"Well, would you be interested in working full-time as a cook for me? You would learn to make every low-sodium recipe in the book."

She laughed. "If only I had some actual experience cooking professionally, I would love it."

"Well, you've been getting plenty of experience this past week. As far as I've seen, you seem to be handling it perfectly well. Everyone loves your food, there have been no complaints – which is a rarity – and I've seen you while you are cooking. You look happy."

She realized that he was serious. "Are you really offering me a job?"

"If you want it, it's yours. I will have to clear it with the board, but I don't see why they would disapprove. The job description requires experience in the kitchen, but it doesn't say how much, and as I said, you have already proven yourself."

"Wow. I... can I have time to think about it?"

"Of course. Just let me know what you decide. I think you would be a good match for the position, but if you would rather work somewhere else, I completely understand."

She fell silent, looking at her menu as an excuse to be alone with her thoughts for a few minutes. The job offer had come as a complete surprise. Why had he done it? She really didn't have any experience in a professional kitchen, other than the volunteer work that she had done for the past week. He was going out on a limb for her, and he didn't even know her that well. Was he offering her the job because he thought she would be good at it, or because he was interested in her? It was a lot to think about, and she wanted to talk it over with Alicia first before deciding.

Deciding to turn the conversation away from herself, she asked Nick about his job. "What made you decide to start working there? Did you move to town for the position?"

"Well, like I said, I've seen the way that some of these places are run. My own grandmother was in one that wasn't great. A lot of these people, well, they don't really have anyone else in their lives. This is the end of the road for them, and if I can make the last months or years a little bit better, I'm happy to do so. It may not be what I thought I would want to do when I was a kid, but I'm happy here, and I don't think I would want to do anything else now. And yes, I moved to town for the job. The position opened up just as I was wanting to move. It was like it was meant to be."

"I think it's wonderful when people are passionate about their jobs," she said. As she spoke, she realized that she had never worked a job that *she* was passionate about. She liked the grocery store, but she wasn't crazy about the work itself. Working as a cook at the assisted living home, while it might not be the glamorous restaurant she had imagined as a child, she would be doing something that she actively enjoyed. She shook her head, not wanting to decide on the spot either way. She would go home and talk to Alicia about it, and come back to it later. Nick didn't seem in a big rush to hire someone before the end of the year, so she wouldn't be in a hurry either.

CHAPTER TWELVE

As Christmas got closer, she had less and less time to think about Nick and his offer. She saw him in passing when she was at the assisted living home, but both of them had their hands full doing their jobs. Christmas season was prime time for visiting, and there was a seemingly endless stream of people who were anxious to make sure that their family members were being taken care of. She often had to make extra for dinner, just to accommodate all of the guests. She was glad that they were visiting their families, but it certainly made more work for her and everybody else.

She woke up earlier than usual on Christmas morning, filled with excitement even though it had been many years since she had woken up as a child to run downstairs and find gifts under the Christmas tree. She had always loved this holiday, though, and was looking forward to even her own small celebrations.

She got out of bed, putting on her favorite soft bathrobe and walking downstairs to let Frankie outside. Snow had fallen overnight, but the sky was clear now, and the fresh snow in the backyard glittered. After Frankie was done, Autumn gave her her breakfast – which was the best present in the world as far as the dog was concerned – and made herself a cup of coffee, to which she added a dash of peppermint extract in addition to the usual sugar and milk. Feeling content, she walked back into the living room and sipped her coffee while she listened to Christmas carols on the radio. At nine, she picked up the phone and called her mother, who lived half a continent away.

"Merry Christmas, Mom," she said.

"Merry Christmas, Autumn. How are you doing? I hope you aren't spending the day alone. I'm going to try to fly out to visit next year."

"I'll be spending the evening with Uncle Albert and Aunt Lucy," she told her mother. "I might stop and visit Alicia later today. For now, it's just me and Frankie, but that's okay."

"I miss you so much, sweetie. We have to have Christmas together one of these years. I love you."

"I love you too, Mom. We'll see each other soon. It's been too long already."

After getting off the phone with her mother, she called her sister and had a similar conversation. Michelle put her three-year-old daughter on the line, and Autumn chatted with her niece for a few minutes.

"She loves the gift you sent her," her sister said, taking the phone back. "Thank you, Autumn. You have got to come and visit sometime."

"I will," Autumn promised. "Once things settle down here, I will drive out there for the weekend."

Feeling the first spark of loneliness that she had felt since waking up, she said her goodbyes and hung up. How had her family ended up so far apart? She missed them all. Once upon a time, they had been close, but now they were all so focused on their own lives that they hardly seemed to have time for each other.

Deciding it was time for her own Christmas celebration, she put down her mug of coffee and knelt by the small tree that she had set up in the corner by the fireplace. There were a couple of presents that she had wrapped herself the night before. Two of them were for Frankie. She called the dog over and unwrapped the gifts, giving her a new squeaker toy and a couple of treats from the new package that she had bought. Then she turned to the small gift that she bought for herself; a pair of socks with Cairn terriers on them. It wasn't much, but she wasn't comfortable spending her own money on an extravagant gift for herself, especially not when her own financial situation was in such dire straits.

"Merry Christmas, Frankie," she said to the dog. "I'm glad you're here with me."

The dog, who was busy tearing up the discarded wrapping paper, didn't look up, but her tail wagged harder. Autumn smiled. She may not have a loved one to spend the day with, but that didn't mean that she had to be lonely. She had her dog and herself, and even though they lived hundreds of miles apart, she knew that her family was there for her in spirit.

A little bit before noon, she got dressed for the day and left the house, making sure Frankie was settled in with her new toy to keep her occupied. She had a bag of gifts for Alicia and Rory, who she was planning to visit before she headed to the assisted living home to start on dinner.

Her friend gave her a hug when she got to the door and invited her in. Their house already smelled wonderful; Alicia had gotten an early start on Christmas dinner. Her friend offered her a small glass of wine, and they sat in the living room chatting for a good twenty minutes before Autumn excused herself.

"I should get going," she said. "I have to get started on dinner. We are eating earlier than usual, and there will be quite a few people there. The staff will be eating the Christmas dinner too, and a lot of relatives will be visiting."

"I just love that you're volunteering there," Alicia said. "You seem to enjoy it so much. As a plus, you get to see Nick a lot."

"I don't talk to him much while I'm there," she admitted. "He's working. I don't want to distract him."

"How have things gone since your date?"

"Good," Autumn said. "He's always very friendly, and he said that he wants to go out again. I told him after the holidays are over would probably be best."

"Why do you want to wait so long?"

"I have just been busy at the store, and working at Asheville Meadows in the evenings, and I'm sure he's busy himself too. I've also been job searching, of course."

"You don't think you're going to take his offer?"

"I don't know," Autumn said. "I don't know if he's offering me the job because he really thinks I would be good at it, or if he's just doing it because he likes me and wants to do something nice. I don't want to take it for the wrong reasons, and I don't want to get him into trouble with the Board of Directors if I'm not up to the task." She looked at the clock. "I really have to get going. I don't think I will decide until after Christmas. We can talk about this more later."

It was wonderful to walk into the assisted living home. Nearly every inch of the interior was covered with decorations; there were paper snowflakes that the residents had made, beautiful lights, and two large Christmas trees in the main area. Having been there so much over the past couple of weeks, Autumn had gotten to know many of the residents and staff quite well, and people greeted her warmly when she arrived.

Just being there made her heart feel glad. She hung her coat and her purse in the office on one of the hooks, then went to find Natalie, who would be helping her make Christmas dinner.

"There you are," she said when she found the girl at last. "Are you ready to get started?"

"Yes, just let me take Mrs. Zimmer to the common room. I'll meet you in the kitchen."

Autumn hurried to the kitchen, eager to get started. She poured over the menu, making sure she didn't miss anything. She had already gone over it a couple of times, but wanted to get everything right. Pot roast would be the main course, with fruit salad, homemade bread, and a variety of pies for dessert. They usually served frozen dinner rolls instead of homemade bread, but tonight was special. Everything would be made from scratch. It was going to be a busy day, but she was glad that all of the residents here would be getting a wonderful homemade meal for Christmas.

She decided to start by preparing vegetables for the pot roast. She was busy peeling carrots when Natalie appeared in the kitchen doorway.

"Ms. Roth, someone is here to see you."

"Who?" she asked, surprised. If it was Nick, he would have just walked into the kitchen.

"Brandon... I can't remember his last name. I'm sorry."

Brandon was there? What in the world could he want? She hadn't spoken with him since he had stopped by her house the week before her date with Nick. Hoping that everything was okay, she took off her apron and told Natalie to keep working on the vegetables.

She found Brandon waiting in the common room. He was holding a bouquet of roses, which he handed over to her when he saw her.

"They're beautiful," she said, "What is this about, Brandon?"

"I want to apologize. I know our last discussion didn't go so well. The more I think about it, the surer I am; I made a mistake, Autumn. I know that it will probably take you a while to trust me again, and I want to make it up to you. You are a wonderful person, who I want to be a part of my life for a long time to come."

He pulled her into a hug. She returned it, feeling flustered. She opened her eyes, and over Brandon's shoulder, she saw Nick. He was staring at the two of them, a hurt expression on his face.

CHAPTER THIRTEEN

She pulled back, out of Brandon's embrace. She didn't know if things would go anywhere with Nick, but she wanted to give it a chance. Just one date with him had shown her that there was so much more out there. She cared about Brandon, yes, but things were over between them. He had to accept that.

"Brandon, I appreciate the gesture, but you really shouldn't have come here. I have a job to do, and I have to get back to work. What I said before still stands. I think you were correct when you said that we aren't right for each other. Maybe we can get a coffee sometime this week and talk about it, but I really do have to go now. I hope you have a wonderful Christmas."

"That's it?" he said. "Autumn, I miss you so much. I haven't been able to stop thinking about you. Please, give me one more chance. I…"

Autumn heard a soft *whump* come from behind her, then heard someone start screaming. She spun around and realized that the sounds had come from the kitchen. Dropping the roses, she rushed forward. She found Natalie beating a fire out of her smoking apron. Her hair was singed, as was her shirtsleeve, and her hand and arm were burned. The oven door was open, and a lighter lay on the floor.

"Natalie, what happened?" she asked, kneeling beside the younger woman.

"I don't know," Natalie sobbed. "I was trying to get the oven lit – the pilot light must've gone out – but when I clicked the lighter on, a huge fireball just exploded. Thank goodness I was using one of those long lighters, or my entire head would be on fire."

"We have to get out of the kitchen now," Autumn said. "Someone go and find Nick I think he's in his office."

No matter what he said, she knew that she would no longer entertain the thought that all of this was a coincidence. Someone is trying to kill whoever cooked in the kitchen at the assisted living home.

"What happened?"

She turned to see Brandon standing in the doorway to the kitchen.

"You should get going. We can deal with this," she said.

"No, I want to help," he said.

"What's going on?"

Nick was there now, standing next to Brandon, gazing at Natalie with concern.

"Someone fixed the oven so it would explode when someone tried to light it," Autumn said.

His eyes widened. "Both of you need to get out of here right now," he said. "We don't know if there are other booby-traps in here. I'm going to call the police, but for now, we need to keep everyone out of the kitchen."

She helped Natalie into the common area, and one of the other staff members brought an ice pack for her. The sight of the injured young employee brought both residents and staff swarming over, making sure she was okay and asking what had happened.

Autumn saw a couple of people heading towards the kitchen, their faces curious. She got up and hurried over to the door.

"No one can go inside," she said. "I'm sorry, but it may not be safe."

Mrs. Zimmer, who was standing by the door with her walker, was frowning.

"You really have bad luck, don't you?" she said.

"It's not bad luck," Autumn said. "Someone's trying to sabotage me."

She managed to shoo people away from the door. By now, the common room was full of people. Everyone was talking about what had happened and crowding around Natalie. Feeling frazzled, Autumn took a step toward Natalie, but Brandon beat her there. She saw him ask people to give the young woman space, and offered him a smile from across the room. With Natalie taken care of, she had to find Nick.

He was in his office, and was just getting off the phone with the police when she found him. "They're on their way," he said. "I asked for an ambulance too. I don't know how hurt Natalie is."

"Good. I can't believe something like this happened again. Who had access to the kitchen today?"

"Too many people," he said. "It's been a crazy day. Natalie helped make lunch with a couple of the other staff members. I don't know who made breakfast. The door has been open most of the day; Natalie was trying to clean it for you so that it would be nice for Christmas dinner. A couple of the residents were also in there, making Christmas cookies for their families. It could've been anyone. I know you're going to hate to hear this, but are you sure it wasn't an accident?"

"How could this have been an accident?"

"Well, it's possible that the pilot light just went out. It does happen sometimes, and these ovens are older."

"If that was the case, wouldn't the gas have shut off automatically? There should be a safety valve, shouldn't there?"

"There is, but it responds to the metal cooling down after the pilot light goes out. The gas would have kept flowing for a little bit. Like I said, it's an older system and it isn't perfect. The fact that the explosion was so small tells me that the valve did work. The gas must have shut off just a few minutes after the pilot light went out."

Autumn sighed and took a seat across from him. "So you think that it was an accident, just like the burners being left on and Benson's EpiPen disappearing?"

"I don't know what I think," he said. "That's why I called the police. It's just hard to imagine that someone would try to kill the cook on Christmas day. What motive could anyone have to try to kill you and Natalie?"

Autumn frowned. Something had occurred to her. Natalie had been around each time that something bad had happened. This most recent incident was the least serious; like Nick had said, the emergency shut off valve had worked, and the explosion had been minor. Was it possible that she had done this on purpose to turn suspicion away from herself? If so, did that mean that she had something else planned?

She shook her head. No, that was ridiculous. Natalie had never given Autumn any reason not to trust her. Besides, why would the young staff member want her out of the kitchen?

"The police will be here soon," he said after a moment. "And the ambulance for Natalie. We should talk to them together."

"What are we going to do about Christmas dinner?"

"Well, with any luck, they will be able to finish up their investigation soon and we can get back to cooking. I'll help you out; now that Natalie is injured, I wouldn't want to ask anyone else to do it."

It took the police a while to get through the kitchen and make sure everything else was safe. Natalie left for the hospital to get her burns treated, and everyone in the assisted living home wished her well. Brandon insisted on staying, and Autumn did her best to ignore him. She wished that he would just listen to her and leave; he was choosing the wrong time to act chivalrous.

At last, the police determined that the kitchen was safe. They had been unable to find any evidence of foul play. They suggested to Nick that he implement some basic safety training for anyone who was working in the kitchen, then left.

"Are you willing to help me with dinner?" Nick asked her. "I don't want you to stay if you feel unsafe. No one will blame you if you don't want to cook anymore."

"I'll stay," she said with a sigh. "I wouldn't feel right leaving, not with my aunt and uncle here, and not with you here. I would feel terrible if someone else got hurt."

"All right, let's get to work. Dinner might be a bit late, but I think we still have time. Do you want to ask your boyfriend to help?"

"Brandon? We aren't dating. We broke up a while back. I don't know what he's doing here, but I already told him I'm not interested."

His face seemed to relax a bit. He gave her a small smile. "Do you want me to ask him to leave?"

She glanced through the kitchen door, where she saw Brandon talking with her uncle and helping her aunt drink a glass of water.

"No," she said. "They like him, and he's a good guy. Let him stay if he wants to. I don't think he has anywhere else to go, anyway. His family all lives out of town."

Nick nodded, and the two of them began work on Christmas dinner. Even though she was jumpy, nothing else happened. It seemed that the police had been right; there were no further booby-traps in the kitchen.

A couple of hours later, Autumn pulled the freshly baked bread out of the oven with a feeling of deep satisfaction. Despite everything that had happened, she and Nick had managed to pull together a wonderful Christmas dinner.

After the bread had had a few minutes to cool, she began to cut it into slices. Eager to try a bite of her creation, she cut a small slice for herself. She buttered it, then raised the warm bread to her lips.

A moment later, she spit the bite out in disgust.

CHAPTER FOURTEEN

"What's wrong?" Nick asked, turning to her with concern on his face. His sleeves were rolled up, and he had an apron tied around his waist.

"It's salty," she said. "Way too salty."

Frowning, he tasted a piece of the bread himself, and spit it out immediately. "How did this happen?"

She had no answers. Worried, they tasted everything. The pot roast and fruit salad were both fine, but the gravy and the pie crusts were all way too salty.

"There must be something wrong with the flour," he said.

She pulled the bag of flour out of the pantry and tasted a tiny bit. She could tell immediately what was wrong. Granules of salt had been mixed in with the flour.

"Okay," she said, "this cannot be an accident. Nick, you have to admit that something is going on here."

He gazed at the flour, and she saw sadness on his face. "You're right. But who? Who would do this? Why would someone want you out of the kitchen so badly? Why kill Benson?"

"I don't know," she said. "Whatever's going on, it has to have something to do with the job position, doesn't it? Whoever is doing this doesn't seem to be targeting anyone in particular. We should start looking through the applications."

"All right. We've got about half an hour before everyone will be ready. Let's leave the food on warmers, and go to my office. We can look at the applications together. I don't want to involve the police in this until after dinner, though. Everyone's looking forward to this dinner so much. We will just have to put some frozen rolls in the oven and use one of the gravy mixes."

"Agreed. Let's go look now, though. I won't feel safe until we know who it is."

They returned to his office, shutting the door behind them. He pulled the blinds shut, then took a stack of papers out of the drawer, handing her half.

"You start with these, I'll take the other half. Look for people that live locally, or have relatives in the home. Whoever did this would've had to have been here all three days that something happened."

They began pouring through the applications. Autumn cross-referenced the names with the names of the residents, and looked for any possible connection between them. There weren't too many applications, and it didn't take long until one of them found something promising.

"Look at this," he said. "Jimmy Zimmer. He applied before Cook Benson died. That's a bit suspicious, isn't it?"

"That's *very* suspicious," she said.

"We were looking for a temporary cook, since our other cook is out on maternity leave, so it may not mean anything, but look at this... He applied again a few days after Cook Benson died. We should talk to his grandmother and see if she can tell us anything. She might remember where he was on those days."

Taking the application, Nick left the room. Autumn followed him, wondering if this could really be it.

Had this Jimmy person tried to kill her? Just how badly could he want the job?

Nick stopped outside of Mrs. Zimmer's room. He knocked on the door, and said, "Mrs. Zimmer? It's Mr. Holt. I'd like to speak to you for a second."

"Come on in," she called faintly. He pushed open the door and Autumn followed him. Ms. Zimmer was sitting on her chair, reading a book.

"Can we sit down?" Nick asked her. She nodded, and the two of them sat on the couch.

"We just want to ask you some questions about your grandson. He sent a couple applications in for the job as the new cook. He seems pretty interested in the job. Could you tell me anything about him?"

"Oh, yes. He's always wanted to cook. He is so skilled in the kitchen. He always made the best meals for us. I practically raised him, you know. He lost his job a couple of months ago, poor thing, and has been searching so hard ever since."

Nick exchanged a look with Autumn. That could be motive, right there.

"Mrs. Zimmer, do you know if your grandson was here earlier today?"

"Why yes, he stopped in to give me my gift, and he told me he would be back later for dinner."

"Do you remember if he visited the Sunday that Benson passed away?"

"He was there for dinner…" She trailed off. "Now, Mr. Holt, I'm sure I'm wrong about this, but it sure sounds to me like you are accusing him of something."

Nick opened his mouth, but at that moment the door to the room opened. In walked a man about

Autumn's age. He looked between his grandmother and Nick.

"Is everything all right?" he asked.

"Oh, Jimmy, I'm glad you're here. This man is making a horrible accusation."

"You're accusing my grandmother of something?" Jimmy asked, his face reddening. "How dare you? You are just like all of the other homes out there, trying to take advantage of the elderly."

"Now, Mr. Zimmer – can I call you Jimmy? I…"

"No, I don't want to hear it. As soon as I get a job, I'm taking my grandmother out of here."

"Jimmy, they aren't accusing me," the older woman said. "They were accusing you."

Jimmy froze. "What?"

"It's just, a few things have come to our attention. We know that you were here earlier today, and that you were there when Benson passed away. I don't want to upset you, but I am going to insist that you talk to the police. I'm sure this is all a big misunderstanding, but I have to do my best to protect the people here, and whoever has been sabotaging the kitchen is putting everyone in danger."

"You think I hurt those people?" he asked, looking stunned. "I would never hurt anyone, not for a stupid job like this. I don't even want to work here anymore, not after this."

"I'm sorry, Jimmy, but you are going to need to calm down. I am going to call the police."

"Nick, wait," Autumn said. She had spotted something on Mrs. Zimmer's messy desk. Two syringes with the word epinephrine on them. Nick followed her gaze, then they both turned to look at Mrs. Zimmer.

"What is this? This is insane." Jimmy made a fist and took a step closer. He hadn't seen their look. Nick rose, tensing.

"Enough," the older woman said. "Jimmy didn't do anything."

"I know he didn't, Mrs. Zimmer," he said. "I got this all wrong, didn't I?"

"What's going on?" Jimmy said, looking between them.

"I did it, Jimmy. I did it for you and your family, so you would have a nice job to take care of them."

"W-what? Gramma, don't say things like that. You don't have to protect me. I'm innocent."

"I did it, Jimmy. I knew Benson was allergic to peanut butter, so I sprinkled a little bit of the powder in his drink. I took away those syringes, and hid the keys. I thought if he left, it would give you the opening you needed to get this job. You've always dreamed of having your own kitchen, Jimmy. You could have cooked for me every day."

"Did you do the burners on the stove, too? That almost killed me," Autumn said.

"I would have been sorry if you died, dear, but Jimmy is my family. I'm not going to be around much longer, and spending the rest of my life in prison wouldn't be the end of the world if it meant my grandson would be able to support his wife and child. I'm sorry poor Natalie got hurt, but it sounds like she will be just fine."

"And the salt in the flour?" Nick said.

"I figured if everything else failed, you might be asked to leave if you wrecked Christmas dinner."

Jimmy stared at his grandmother. "I can't believe this," he said. "You did this? You hurt those people? You killed someone?"

"It was for you, dear. You need the work so badly, and I knew that if this man just gave you a chance, you would impress him."

Nick was shaking his head. "Mrs. Zimmer, please stay in your seat. Autumn, would you call the police? I need to keep an eye on her."

"I will." Autumn rose, and edged around Jimmy, who was staring at his grandmother in horror. She hurried to the office and got her phone out of her coat pocket. She dialed 911, and waited anxiously for someone to answer. The kitchen saboteur had been discovered, but she found herself wishing that Nick had been right and it had all been a string of coincidences. Her heart was broken for Jimmy. Maybe his grandmother's mind wasn't as clear as it once had been, but there was no getting around the fact that in trying to help him, she had killed one person, and had nearly killed others.

EPILOGUE

Autumn sat down at the table with her aunt and uncle. They each had plates of pot roast in front of them, with bowls of fruit salad, and piping hot dinner rolls. In the kitchen, two pans of chocolate cake were cooling; she would have to go and frost them in a few minutes. With chocolate icing, warm caramel sauce, and vanilla ice cream, it might not be as traditional as pumpkin pie, but it would still make for a delicious dessert. She thought they had done well, considering what they had been forced to deal with.

They were the only ones who knew what had happened. The other residents hadn't been told yet. She and Nick had discussed it, and had decided to let them enjoy Christmas with their families. They would address the issue the next day. As some of the surprise over who the culprit was wore off, Autumn realized that she should have made the connection sooner. Mrs. Zimmer had been there each time that something had happened. If only she had been a little quicker on the uptake, Natalie might not have been injured.

Nick wasn't completely without blame either. He had been in denial that the incidents were linked. If he had simply looked a little harder, he might have discovered Mrs. Zimmer before she got the chance to hurt anyone else.

In the end, Autumn knew that both of them could have done better, but it wasn't either of their faults. She would drive herself crazy if she blamed herself for this. The important thing was, Mrs. Zimmer had been caught, and wouldn't be hurting anyone else.

On the upside, Brandon had finally left. She had the feeling that her Uncle Albert had something to do with it, but she didn't bring it up at the table. She felt bad for Brandon, but she didn't want to get back together with him. He wasn't right for her, and she wasn't right for him. It was time that they both found their own ways without each other.

She hadn't seen Nick since the police had taken the older woman away. She thought that he might have retreated to his office. She knew that the incident with Mrs. Zimmer had saddened him deeply. He cared about everyone he was responsible for, and had tried extremely hard to convince himself that none of his residents or staff were to blame. She hoped that he would come to terms with things soon, and not blame himself for too long.

"Don't look so gloomy, dear," her Uncle Albert said. "This is Christmas, it's a time to be happy. Your aunt and I are thrilled that you're having Christmas dinner with us. You did a marvelous job. The pot roast is great. I'm sorry that there was a mishap with the bread, but no one will complain about the dinner rolls once they learn what happened."

"Thanks, Uncle Albert," she said. "Merry Christmas. I'm glad I get to spend it with the two of you too."

"Merry Christmas," he replied, smiling at her. Her aunt, unable to speak, patted her arm instead and gave her a lopsided smile. Unable to imagine how frustrating it must be to be unable to speak, she gave her aunt's hand an extra squeeze.

"I love both of you, you know that, right? There's nowhere I would rather be."

"You know the funny thing?" her Uncle Albert said. "There's nowhere I would rather be either. If you would have asked me five years ago if I wanted to spend Christmas in an assisted living facility, I would've probably had a heart attack from laughing so hard, but right now I just feel lucky that I get to spend it with my wonderful wife and my niece. The people here are good people, and it has really started to feel like home to us. Part of that is thanks to you, Autumn."

"I know what you mean," Autumn said. "This town has really become home to me, too. I'm going to do everything I can to stay here, even though the store will be shutting down."

She knew that she was going to take Nick's offer. Her uncle was right. This assisted living home was a good place, and the people here were like family to her. She would keep working at Green River Grocery until it closed, and then she would come here to start her new job, and her new life. Just a few weeks ago, she had thought that her life was falling apart before her eyes, but now she felt the beginnings of hope. She had a chance to start a new career, one that she was excited about, and she hadn't made what might have been the mistake of her life in getting engaged to Brandon. She only had one life, and she didn't want to just live it, she wanted to enjoy it, and make the world a better place while she did.

Made in the USA
Middletown, DE
21 March 2022

62984821R00095